A Fairytale Christmas

LACY WILLIAMS

ISBN: 1-942505-15-9
ISBN-13: 978-1-942505-15-0

THE COWBOY FAIRYTALES SERIES

A FAIRYTALE CHRISTMAS

"Your highness, this way. With a smile, please!"

Queen Eloise of Glorvaird obediently turned toward the approved royal photographer. But since they'd been at this for over two hours, her smile felt stretched thin. The small body in her arms was wriggling, making it hard to keep the eighteen-month-old boy still.

Cody's hand was warm at her lower back. "Almost done," he murmured. Having her conscientious husband near made the holiday PR event bearable. Almost.

The camera flashed, adding to the spots already blurring her vision. So many photos. Her face was starting to burn, which meant her scars would be on display.

A shriek from her niece Penny drew Eloise's gaze—and everyone else's—to the toddler, who was having a tug-of-war with another little girl over a stuffed bear.

"I think she's had enough," Mia said, bending to scoop up her daughter.

"I think we all have." Cody escorted the

photographer from the huge family-style living room, decorated for the season, at the Glorvaird orphanage. Her husband shook hands with the man and the photographer seemed especially grateful to accept a red and green envelope and a pat on the back.

The small boy in her arms wiggled again, turning his face up to Eloise. "Down," he said with a serious expression.

She set his feet on the floor. He was off in an instant, and the other orphans, released from having to sit still for the photoshoot, rushed the Christmas tree in the corner, shrieking with glee.

Gideon, Eloise's brother-in-law, stood nearby dressed as Santa. He was almost toppled by the crazy children.

Good. They deserved to be spoiled, even if it was only for one day. The orphans occupied a soft spot in Eloise's heart. She wished they could all find homes.

Cody rejoined her as she faded into a shadowed corner, taking a seat on the sofa. She hated the itchy, high-necked dress her stylist had chosen. She'd have chosen something more casual, slacks and a soft blouse, but her PR team had out-voted her.

It was tradition for the royals to spend Christmas Eve at the orphanage, but the event had never been publicized. Not until this year. Alessandra and Gideon, Mia and Ethan with their Penny, and Kylie and Nick were all here. Even Pieter attended this year for the photoshoot.

Without the little orphan boy, Eloise's arms felt

so...empty. She needed a distraction.

"Did you tip the photographer?" she asked.

Cody shrugged.

"Or should I ask, 'how much did you tip the photographer?'"

He linked their fingers together, his handsome face easing into a smile. "It's Christmas."

"He just got an exclusive with the royal family," she pointed out. "He didn't need a bonus."

He shrugged again, his eyes on the action nearer the tree. He chuckled when Penny got right in the middle of the kids. Mia and Ethan's daughter was a rascal who charmed everyone she came in contact with—children and adults alike.

Since Eloise and Cody had married two years ago, he'd taken it upon himself to make her life easier with the press. Between Cody and Jill, who'd proven to be the PR jewel her father had promised, the royal family's relationship with the press had improved a thousand percent. So she let his little parting gift to the photographer pass without a fuss.

He leaned closer to her, slipping his arm around her waist unobtrusively. Although the photographer had left, there were several of the staff from the orphanage still present, and they had to present themselves with royal decorum.

Penny broke from the gaggle of children and ran to them. "Auntie Eloise, Mama said Saint Nick is coming *tonight!*"

"That's right," she said with a laugh. "But he will only bring gifts for little girls who've been good. I heard you threw a tantrum for your daddy yesterday."

The little girl's face drooped. "Aw..." Her face brightened. "But what if I ask daddy to write Saint Nick a note and tell him how good I been all the rest of the year?"

Eloise had to stifle a giggle.

Cody cleared his throat. "That'd probably work, kiddo."

Distracted by a shout from across the room, Penny ran off without a goodbye.

Eloise's smile lingered. Her niece was as effervescent as she remembered Mia being as a young child.

Cody leaned close, tilting his head down to her. "You know, we could have one of our own by next Christmas."

Eloise's breath caught. She tried for a pleasant expression, kept her eyes focused on the children. "Hmm."

"Hmm, *I'll think about it,* or hmm, *quit bringing it up?*"

She felt the tremble in her smile and worked to form her lips into a straight line. Not a frown, because he would know a frown meant she was upset.

She wasn't upset.

She shrugged, and thankfully, he dropped it, distracted by her cousin Pieter, who approached and asked about the Christmas day celebration they'd planned for the royal family. A private celebration, thank goodness.

Several times over the last few months, Cody had hinted at his desire to have children. He hadn't come out and said it outright. As the ruling royal of their kingdom, she was expected to have at least one child, preferably several children, the oldest of whom would inherit the royal title.

She just wasn't ready.

She'd had a difficult relationship with her father, who'd always put the crown above his family. She was desperate not to make the same mistakes.

More than that, though, nearly every time she looked in the mirror, she saw the scars from the auto accident she'd survived—barely—nearly two decades ago. And she imagined what a child—her child—would think when they looked upon her face.

Adults had been disgusted by her scars before. Thank God Cody somehow saw past her looks to the person she was inside.

What if her child felt disgust when they looked at her? Thought her monstrous?

How could she start a family when there was a good chance her own children might think she was a beast?

McKenna Hastings hustled to set the silver tray on the long sideboard draped in white. It seemed as if the wood should be groaning with the amount of food piled on. She'd never seen so much bounty.

The Glorvaird castle was amazing. This room was amazing. Along with the sideboard, the informal family room had two small circular tables surrounded by chairs, along with a couple of expensive-looking couches in a cluster. A tree bigger than McKenna's apartment took up the entire corner of the room and was a little close to the stone fireplace for her comfort, but she figured someone was watching to make sure it didn't burn down, right?

The royal family was due to arrive any minute. They'd just been to visit to the orphanage. It had been two months since she'd seen Pieter, and she couldn't wait to see him. She'd packed a sprig of mistletoe in her suitcase with his name on it, not that it would be needed with the way the castle was decked out. Swags and wreaths of red-ribboned, pungent evergreen boughs decorated walls, staircases, banisters.

A sense of anticipation shivered through her. She had news to share with him about her law school admission. And Pieter had been hinting that he had a surprise for her. He'd said he wanted everything to be perfect this Christmas.

She wasn't sure he'd appreciate finding her in the staff uniform of a black knee-length dress and starched white collar. There'd been a mix-up when she'd arrived hours ago, and she'd gone with it, noticing how stressed the middle-aged housekeeper seemed.

But now she should really go and dress for dinner.

Uh-oh. Seemed it was too late as she heard rumblings from the direction of the front hall. They brought with them a plume of cold air and the smell of snow, and a cacophony of voices.

Silent and quick, the other staff had faded away, all disappearing except for the butler, who would stand by the kitchen door to see to any unmet needs.

Pieter noticed her immediately, his face losing the lines around his mouth and the tightness at the corners of his eyes as his lips spread in an open smile. He headed her way with the cool, panther stride she'd noticed when she'd first met him.

"McKenna, darling." He kissed her swiftly on the mouth and then held her back from him slightly, his hands on her forearms as he looked her up and down. "What are you wearing?"

She tried for a placating smile. "There was a little mix-up in the kitchens, and the head housekeeper thought—"

"Are you joking?" His eyes lit with a flash of temper.

The rest of the royal family had entered the dining room, and Pieter seemed conscious of their presence as he glanced over his shoulder and then lowered his voice. "Tell me she didn't mistake you for a common temp worker."

"I *am* a commoner," she said in her most cheerful voice, hoping to jog him from this mood. She should've escaped from the kitchens sooner to dress, but with the small number of staff on hand, it had been busy.

"It was my fault, really," she said when it seemed her teasing comment was going to do nothing to calm him. "I knew you were going to be at least another hour, and I thought I'd sneak down to the beach you always tell me about, except I got turned around and ended up in the kitchens. The housekeeper was down there with some kitchen staff who were freaking out because a temp worker hadn't shown up, and I got mistaken for her."

And she'd been shoved into a uniform and told to comb back her hair into a neat ponytail before she could blink. She should learn to be more assertive. Hopefully, law school would help her with that.

"Unbelievable." He really should be breathing fire, the way his temper was sparking. "Didn't she look at your hands to see my family crest ring?" He gripped her fingers and raised her hand between them, holding the gold ring so it glinted in the light. Maybe checking that she was still wearing it.

"It wasn't a big deal," she said. "I was happy to help out."

"Not a big deal." Her remark seemed to have made things worse, because he looked off to the side, where the fire had burned down some. His eyes narrowed. "She should be sacked for such impudence."

He seemed more upset than the situation warranted. It wasn't as if she'd missed some big shindig or turned into Cinderella or anything. She'd carried dishes from one place to another.

Now it was her turn to jog his hands, where they were still linked together. "It's Christmas. And, besides, she was stressed about getting the meal put together and served on time. I was happy to help."

Something was noodling through his mind. He still stared at the fireplace, at nothing. A muscle ticked in his jaw, and he carried a fine tension in his shoulders.

She thought of the sweet housekeeper, of her tenderness with the staff, of her care for the family. McKenna was suddenly worried about the woman's job.

"Pieter," she said patiently. "Promise me you won't try to get her fired."

"What? Oh. Fine." He still seemed distracted as she sidled closer and wrapped her arms around his middle. His came naturally around her waist and lower back.

"I've missed you," she murmured, angling for a kiss.

But a little girl's laugh, sounding like a wind chime, stalled her out.

The family had stayed away from her discussion with Pieter, but they'd made a dent in the food on the long table. Gideon and Alessandra already had full plates and were settled on the sofa furthest from the fireplace. Kylie and her husband Nick sat catty-corner to them, chatting with the other couple casually. Eloise and Cody hung back in the entryway, heads bent close in discussion as Mia and Ethan were helping themselves and bobbling an extra plate between them, which must have been for their daughter, the little girl making figure-eights around their feet and trying her best to trip them up.

For a little while, McKenna had forgotten the ball of nerves lodged tightly in her stomach. Pieter had been practically demanding her presence for a Glorvaird Christmas, but she felt unaccountably nervous and out-of-place in the presence of the princesses. And the queen. Don't forget the queen. Maybe being drafted into service for the kitchen staff had been a blessing in disguise, because it had taken her mind off of her nerves for awhile.

For now, she needed a distraction. She latched on to the first thing she could think of. "I've got something big to celebrate over the holiday," she said.

Pieter's gaze went carefully blank. "Do you?"

She nodded, biting her lip. "I got accepted to Purdue. I got the letter before I left home today."

There was the smallest hesitation before his face

creased in a smile, though there was still something of reserve in his expression. "That's wonderful. Everyone, a toast!"

The group went silent and then offered a smattering of applause when Pieter found some champagne glasses and offered a toast for her law school acceptance. Her face flamed the whole time.

He ushered her to the table to make her plate, was conscientious and attentive, but she couldn't help feeling that something was the matter.

Was he missing his mother? She knew they'd always had a contentious relationship, but when the woman had died late last year, Pieter had seemed almost...relieved.

But the holidays could be hard when you were missing someone you loved. She knew that better than anyone.

She'd just have to work to make this a joyful holiday for him anyway.

"Pieter does *not* look happy," Gideon murmured to Alessandra.

His wife snuck an unobtrusive glance to the couch where the prince and his girlfriend sat side-by-side.

It was subtle, but Gideon had grown to recognize the other man's mannerisms and way of carrying himself during the weeks they'd worked together to locate Kylie and keep Pieter's mother from harming her.

Something was definitely bothering the guy.

"Could you overhear what was wrong when we first came in?" she asked.

"Something about the housekeeper thinking McKenna was staff. That would explain the uniform."

"Oh dear." Alessandra's mouth twitched. She stuffed a bite of creamy lobster pasta into her mouth to hide what might be a smile.

"What?"

She shook her head slightly, but he leveled a glance at her. She knew better than to try and keep secrets from him.

She finished chewing and leaned close, whispering in his ear. "Pieter is planning to propose for Christmas. He showed me the ring and everything."

Gideon didn't wince, but he felt for the man. Knowing Pieter, he'd have been counting on the event being perfect. Prince that he was, it was probably hard for him to accept that McKenna had been drafted into service at the palace, even if it was only for a couple of hours.

He spoke in a low voice. "Maybe we'd better defer our *special announcement* until later. We don't want to ruin his big moment."

The food on her plate was almost half-gone, so he wasn't surprised when she daintily set her fork across the edge of the fancy china dish. A staff member in a dress exactly like the one McKenna wore materialized to make the plate disappear and then was gone again.

Alessandra passed one hand unobtrusively over her still-flat stomach. She would be showing before long.

"I don't see how we can keep it a secret much longer," she murmured. "The kitchen staff must already suspect since they've been making me special breakfasts the last two weeks."

Gideon nodded. "You're probably right."

Of course she was right. But he'd enjoyed having the secret just between the two of them. Being a royal was the complete opposite of what his life as a Navy SEAL had been. As a SEAL, everything was covert, kept under wraps, classified. He hadn't even been able to tell his family where he was assigned.

Now, his every move was tracked by the castle staff—so they could support the royal family in any way necessary—and every movement outside the castle was fodder for the public. When the fact that they were expecting was made public, no doubt they'd have paparazzi hounding them constantly, vying to be the first to report news to the public. Just thinking about it made him want to sigh.

It had been wonderful sharing this secret with Alessandra, even if only for a few weeks.

Gideon had been a mixture of elated and terrified when she'd told him she suspected she was pregnant. They hadn't been actively *trying*, but they hadn't been particularly careful either, ready to accept the blessing of an addition to their family whenever it would come.

And here it was.

He would have to video chat with his brother, Matt, and sister, Carrie, back in the States. Or maybe he and Alessandra could invite them to Glorvaird early in the new year to tell them face-to-face. They'd talked of coming over at Christmas, but Gideon's niece, Scarlett, had had a special Christmas production for her ballet class, and Carrie had wanted to be there for it.

"Are you still certain Eloise will be happy for us?" Lately, he'd seen things that made him think his sister-in-law was discontent. A certain expression she'd wear when she watched Penny playing on the floor. Almost a wistfulness.

If Eloise wanted a baby and he and Alessandra were pregnant first, could it cause a rift between the sisters?

"Of course she'll be happy. She was happy for Mia, wasn't she?"

Maybe he was wrong. Maybe he was just overprotective, looking for something to worry about, as there'd been no recent credible threats against the crown.

Just then, Pieter cleared his throat, bringing everyone's attention to him. "I'd like to…"

Before he got any further, a butler appeared in the doorway. "Princess Kylie, your special guests have just arrived."

"What special guests?" her husband Nick asked as she jumped up from her chair, almost spilling her plate from her lap in her exuberance.

"C'mon," she said, tugging on his hand to drag him out of his chair. "Let's go into the front hall to greet them."

"Greet who?" But he followed her with a doting smile.

Meanwhile, Pieter settled back in his seat, face a careful mask. "Never mind."

Kylie couldn't contain her excitement as she ran into the castle's expansive front hall. She saw her sister-in-law, Gentry, first, who stood a little in front of Nick's parents.

She'd wanted to surprise him for Christmas, and it appeared her plan had worked, because the Harrises had arrived without anyone other than Eloise and Kylie's personal assistant, Alyssa, finding out.

She hugged the now fifteen-year-old girl, who was looking around bug-eyed, much like Kylie had done when she'd first visited the castle.

Nick's parents appeared more hesitant than awed. Snow snuck in around their feet as a footman closed the huge entry door behind them.

When she and Gentry turned, their arms still wrapped around each others' waists, Nick froze in the hall.

Kylie could read the surprise on her husband's face. Less evident was the wary expression, one that matched his father's exactly.

"Big brother!" Gentry cried out. She let go of Kylie to rush her brother.

He caught her in a bear hug, a shocked beat of laughter squishing out of him. "What are you doing here, squirt?"

Gentry growled and wriggled in his arms, apparently attempting to find a place to pinch him, but he kept her arms pinned effectively, both of them dissolving into laughter.

"Mr. Harris, Mrs. Harris." She greeted Nick's parents, holding out both hands.

Mrs. Harris accepted her hands, a smile on her face as she looked over Kylie's shoulder to watch her son and daughter roughhousing. "Thank you for inviting us, dear."

Nick's father didn't crack a smile. Mrs. Harris nudged him with her elbow. His eyes slid to Kylie, but he still didn't crack.

"Wasn't it kind of Kylie to pay our way over here so we could be with Nick for Christmas?"

The older man grunted.

"What was that?" Nick asked as he and Gentry joined them. He shot a look to Kylie that told her he'd heard what his mom had said.

"Just saying hello to your parents." Kylie affected her most innocent look.

"Nicky." His mom embraced him, but his dad stood back with arms crossed.

Oh, this was a disaster. She'd prayed so hard for a reconciliation between Nick and his dad. Their relationship had broken down years ago when Nick's ex-girlfriend had conned a bunch of folks—including Mr. Harris—into investing in a fictional mutual fund.

Mr. Harris had lost a huge chunk of his and Mrs. Harris's retirement funds.

Nick hadn't known anything about the fraud, but because of his relationship with the woman who'd perpetrated the fraud, many people in town had blamed him. Especially after she'd left town and he'd stuck around.

And Nick's dad had never forgiven him. Kylie hadn't seen the man in two years—he'd been a reluctant attendee to their wedding—and had hoped that this Christmas, the gift she could give Nick would be reconciliation.

She'd finally found a measure of peace with the memory of her mom. Sure, they'd had their differences and disagreements, but there was only so much bitterness you could hold onto against someone who'd passed on.

Plus, Kylie's mom had been a part of finding her sisters, the family she hadn't known about for almost three decades but that had changed her life for the better. She'd found where she belonged, here in Glorvaird. She and all three sisters had grown close and shared their lives with each other.

Today, reconciliation didn't seem likely for Nick and his father, not with the way Mr. Harris stood standoffish. Why had he come along, if he didn't want to fix things with his son?

She forced a smile. "You three must be hungry after your trip. Supper is still on the table. Come this way, and you can meet my sisters."

Her wedding day to Nick had been such a blur,

she couldn't have said whether his parents had met Eloise and the other princesses or not. The wedding had taken place in a huge, old cathedral nearby. Nick's parents and sister had stayed in the castle, though things had been bustling and busy and then after they'd left on their honeymoon, she didn't know which of the princesses would've play hostess.

Maybe her sisters would be distraction enough from the disaster this was turning out to be.

"You should've let one of the staff put that together for you." Mia looked over the mishmash of small metal parts belonging to the tiny bicycle her husband was attempting to put together.

It was late, and the different segments of the royal family had gone their separate ways. She and her small family had settled into their suite for the night.

It had been Ethan's idea to purchase a small bike with training wheels for Penny, but she hadn't expected this late-night construction project in their sitting room.

"I want to do it myself," he said. Or at least that's what she thought he'd said. He had a flashlight pinched between his lips, aimed at the paper instructions near his bent knee.

"Why don't you turn the lights on?" she asked.

"No way. I don't want to wake her up."

They shared a commiserating glance. Penny was a notoriously light sleeper, and just getting her to sleep in her own bed was a huge accomplishment for them. She still crawled into their bed sometimes in the night and often begged to sleep with them at bedtime.

"Besides, I'm almost done." He went back to the page, tapping a finger on the corner.

The many unattached pieces discounted his statement. The handlebars and seat were attached, but the bike was upside down, and neither wheel was attached.

She sighed. "I'll help."

She sat on the floor next to him and pulled the instruction sheet to herself. "Flashlight. What step are you on?"

He handed her the small flashlight. "Seven. Or F."

She wrinkled her nose.

"Hey, it's not going to fall apart when I'm done with it."

"That remains to be seen."

She handed him the nut and bolt that belonged on the front wheel, nudging his knee as she did.

"Don't critique me too hard. This might be my only time to put a bike together." He said the words casually, and his head remained down, focused on his work.

Her heart squeezed. While getting pregnant had been easy for them, she'd had a difficult last trimester. She'd been ordered to bed rest for several weeks before the birth. And they'd had a scare at the delivery. Or rather, Ethan had had the worst part of the scare as she'd almost slipped away. The doctors had revived her, but it had been a near thing.

After consulting with several physicians who'd

been unanimous in their diagnosis that another pregnancy might kill her, she and Ethan had both agreed that Penny would be their only child.

She just hadn't expected it to hurt so much.

For a while after Penny's birth, Mia had lived in a place of fear and clung tightly to her newborn daughter, content in the decision they'd made.

But now...now...it felt as if their family were incomplete. There was a hole that more children should fill.

"Did you see the little boy who followed Penny around all evening at the orphanage?" She asked the question carefully, not looking at him but focusing on the pieces of metal at her fingertips.

She handed him another nut and bolt, smiling softly when he spun the wheel he'd attached.

"Hard to miss," he said with a quiet chuckle. "She was acting like a little mommy, bossing him around. He seemed to like it, though."

A hot knot rose in Mia's throat. Even Penny sensed that there should be a little brother or sister for her to mother. Mia could imagine it so easily...

Except for the part where she wasn't alive to see her children grow up.

"Have you ever thought about adopting?" he asked.

"Have you?"

He nodded, twisting one last nut and then looking at her. "Some. I wasn't sure how you'd feel after everything, and I didn't want to rush you if you weren't ready to talk about more kids. Or if you'd decided you didn't want more at all."

Her heart panged at the sensitive cowboy. Since the beginning, he'd cared for her needs, always putting her above his own. How had she gotten so lucky?

"Adopting a child—or children—into the royal family would be unprecedented," she said.

He nodded. But his eyes searched her face as if he knew she wasn't finished.

"Of course, three cowboys marrying into the royal family was also unprecedented," she said. "And I shouldn't even mention Kylie."

He grinned. "So you're saying it could be an option?"

She nodded slowly, letting the idea slide over her. It seemed to fill a special notch in her heart. It felt right.

"I'll have to talk to Eloise, of course."

He nodded again. He was so easygoing, her cowboy. Having to get royal approval didn't faze him. Putting up with Mia's occasional mood swing didn't either.

"Are you sure you wouldn't rather wait?" she asked. "You'd talked about going to university, and that got put off because of Penny." And Mia's own fragile health after the birth.

He shrugged. "It's become less important to me. With the staff you've got in place, especially Roberto"—their personal assistant—"I can understand the issues facing the kingdom. I feel I can do my part to help you. There will be years when the children are older that I can go back to school, if it still seems like I need to."

Somehow as they'd been talking, he'd edged closer, or maybe she had. Now their knees bumped, and he leaned even closer, making their shoulders bump as well.

"I love you," he whispered.

"Mmm, me too," she murmured just before their lips met.

"Mommy, Daddy! Mommy, Daddy!"

Ethan pried one eye open as he felt a small torpedo of energy hit the end of the bed.

The digital bedside clock read five-fifteen.

"I just had a very bad dream," Mia muttered.

His arm was wrapped around her waist, and he felt her shift slightly. The bed bounced as Penny crawled from the foot to snuggle between them, dislodging his arm and burrowing into the tiny space between them.

"Santa came! He came!" came the excited squeak. It was accompanied by a wiggle, as if she was so thrilled she couldn't be still.

It was still pitch dark in the room, only a sliver of faint light coming in from where Penny had pushed open their bedroom door.

"It's too early," Mia said, voice rough with sleep.

He couldn't help but smile, remembering several Christmases when it had been just him and his dad, where he'd snuck into his dad's room before the crack of dawn.

"Stop it," Mia complained sleepily, somehow

knowing. "You're encouraging her." But her hand snuck onto his pillow and caressed the hair at his nape tenderly.

He couldn't help it. Having a young child meant seeing Christmas through her eyes, and getting to experience the wonder of it all over again. A few nights ago, they'd allowed Penny to stay up late, and they'd spent an hour walking along the streets in Glorvaird's quaint downtown, looking at the lights displays. The day they'd decorated the tree in the palace's huge atrium, she'd been a ball of energy and had clustered ornaments all along the bottom two feet of the tree.

He loved every second.

Mia and Penny were his family now. He'd lost all contact with his stepbrothers when they'd refused to see him after a judge had removed them from his custody. For a while, he'd mourned the loss of the relationship that could've been. Until Cody had knocked some sense into him. He'd done everything in his power to build a good relationship with his stepbrothers, and they'd refused. Now he poured his focus and attention to the ladies who were his world. And maybe the idea of adding more children through adoption.

"Go back to sleep, you two," Mia mumbled drowsily.

If he could convince Penny to doze off, the three of them might catch another hour or so of sleep.

But their daughter wriggled again. "Presents!"

Penny sat up. He could feel it, even if he couldn't

see her.

"Ethan..." Mia groaned.

But he sat up too. "Presents."

Penny squealed as he picked her up off the bed and bounced her in his arms. For one moment, he buried his nose in her sweet-smelling little-girl curls.

They headed for the parlor, where he and Mia had piled gifts and a half-hidden bike behind the smaller tree they'd chosen for the personal rooms.

"Let's have some breakfast and let Mommy wake up," he murmured to his daughter. Over his shoulder he called out, "You've got fifteen minutes to join us."

He closed the door before the pillow Mia launched could hit them.

Nick woke to an empty bed. Where was she?

It was Christmas morning, and he'd really hoped to spend a sleepy, slow morning in bed with his wife. The royal family would be exchanging gifts at a late lunch.

At least that was what he'd hoped before the surprise Kylie had perpetrated on him last night. His parents and little sister, in Glorvaird for the holiday.

He propped himself up on one elbow and rummaged in the drawer of his nightstand until he found the small wrapped gift he'd chosen for Kylie. Inside was a small white-gold pendant he'd commissioned for her—a representation of the cabin where they'd hidden out when assassins had been targeting her. He wanted to give it to her before they had to put on their nice faces and join the rest of his family. He and Gideon had a special surprise for her during the family Christmas exchange.

Except she was nowhere to be found.

He visited the bathroom—also empty—and made a cursory attempt to tame his bedhead. His sleep T-shirt and flannel pajama pants would have to do as he opened the door from the bedroom and into their private sitting room.

His dad and Kylie were huddled in a quiet conversation. He guessed his fifteen-year-old sister was sleeping in, the childlike excitement of Christmas long gone. No idea where Mom was.

Dad and Kylie had their backs to him, both seated at the small circular table for two in their breakfast nook. Two steaming cups of coffee and a basket of muffins were on the table. So Kylie must've called down to the kitchens. After last night's feast, most of the staff had the day off.

He should really announce his presence, but after the tension on Dad's face last night, he wasn't in any hurry to face the man. So he stayed in the doorway.

"...mysterious amount deposited in my bank account late last year," Dad was saying. "A large amount."

Kylie toyed with the sugar spoon in her cup. "I'm afraid I wouldn't know anything about that."

"I don't want some princess paying me off so I'll forget what bad decisions my son made."

Nick came off the wall, hurt for himself and offended on Kylie's behalf.

But she didn't seem to need his help. "Did you know," she began, cool and collected, "that each member of the royal house of Glorvaird receives a salary? Royals and spouses alike? Do you know why Nick receives compensation?"

Dad shook his head slightly, but even from behind, Nick could see Kylie had piqued his interest.

"When he joined the royal family, Nick took over as head of several committees. He manages the royal healthcare initiative and is a special advisor to the Glorvaird police, along with several other important jobs. The skills that you and Marcia taught him growing up have served him well."

Dad sat silently for a minute. "He didn't learn it from me. His Ma is the people person."

Wasn't that the truth?

Kylie wasn't done. "If Nick chose to make a gift of part of his salary, and I'm not saying he did, he was probably hoping to be absolved of everything that happened before. With Kara and your money."

His dad was silent for another long moment. Big talker, his pops. "What happened with that girl wasn't his fault. He don't owe me nothin'."

Kylie laid her hand on his dad's forearm. "I lost my mom a little over three years ago. I would do anything to spend one more Christmas with her."

Nick could hear the raw hurt in her voice. He wanted to go to her, but he held back a little longer. She hadn't mentioned her mom in a while, and he'd wondered if she'd been missing her, but hadn't brought it up. Now he had his answer. Hopefully, it would make the gift he and Gideon had found for her that much more poignant.

Kylie went on. "The reason I invited you here was because the best Christmas present I can give Nick would be for the two of you to come to an understanding about what happened."

His heart thumped. Kylie had done a lot of

organizing to get his family here. And he was tired of this rift between himself and his dad. It was time to do something about this.

He came off the door, clearing his throat as he did so. Kylie's and Dad's heads turned toward him.

"For what it's worth, I'm sorry for my part in what happened. I should've been more suspicious of Farah when she wanted details about all of the people in my life." That apology wasn't comfortable, but it was done. It was up to Dad to accept it.

Dad came out of his chair, one hand remaining on the chair back. "It wasn't your fault, son. Everybody in town saw how that girl broke your heart. I guess she blindsided all of us. It's just hard…to have lost so much."

That might be as close to forgiveness as his dad could come. And Nick would take it. He moved forward, and Dad met him halfway in a man-hug, complete with backslaps.

He met Kylie's beaming gaze over Dad's shoulder. Just then, Mom and Gentry came tumbling out of the second bedroom in the suite, both vying for coffee and ratcheting the noise up by a decibel or so.

And ratcheting up the joy in his heart.

Kylie had been right. This Christmas would forever be special to him. His dad was back in his life.

Alessandra came down the long, curved staircase in the castle's foyer. She'd been nauseated and hadn't wanted to join the family until she felt better. And she'd sent Gideon ahead because he was fairly bouncing with anticipation about some gift he and Nick had gotten for Kylie. Also, he'd mumbled something about checking on Pieter on his way out the door.

She couldn't help but be amused by his interest in her cousin. He had been incredibly suspicious of Pieter in the beginning, as Pieter's now-deceased mother had been mentally unstable and at one point had hired assassins to target Alessandra's family. But when Gideon and Pieter had spent several weeks together in the States trying to locate Kylie—who hadn't known she was a princess at the time—they'd forged something of an alliance. It helped that the threat was long gone.

Although she wouldn't say that Gideon and Pieter were best friends, the fact that her husband was worried about Pieter's holiday proposal said enough in itself.

Now she could hear the rumble of voices from the family gathered in the atrium around the grandiose Christmas tree. As she entered the room, she saw Ethan and Mia sitting on the floor, Mia holding Penny on her lap as the three giggled about something. Kylie and Nick and Nick's family were gathered on the opposite side of the tree. The brother and sister seemed to be having an animated discussion. Eloise and Cody were seated together on a settee in between the two other families. There was a fine tension coiled in Eloise's shoulders, though she spoke kindly with McKenna, who was seated on a settee nearby. And there was Pieter, in conversation with Gideon near the door. Her cousin had that same tension he'd carried last night—nervous anticipation, maybe—and since there didn't appear to be a sparkly ring on McKenna's finger, the proposal must not have happened yet.

"There you are." Gideon reached for her and wrapped his arm gently around her waist. He didn't ask after her condition verbally, but she felt his tender perusal anyway.

"I hope everyone wasn't waiting on me." She smiled at Pieter and didn't acknowledge Gideon's subtle worry. There were at least seven months left in her pregnancy. He was going to have to get used to her being slightly under the weather.

Eloise rose and greeted her with a kiss, and the others murmured *hellos* and *Merry Christmases* as Gideon settled her on a settee between Eloise and where Mia and Ethan sat on the floor. Pieter joined

McKenna on the sofa.

Of course they let the impatient three-year-old go first, and Penny tore into her gifts with abandon, making everyone laugh at her antics.

Alessandra opened a beautiful hand-knitted scarf from McKenna and a pair of dazzling diamond earrings from her sister Mia. She was distracted from the pile of gifts at her feet when Gideon nudged her knee.

He jerked his chin toward Kylie, and Alessandra saw her half-sister opening a package wrapped in bright, shiny red paper.

"What is it?" Kylie asked her husband, who was leaning close, watching avidly. It must've been a rhetorical question, because she was still ripping into the package.

She folded back the paper and revealed a small stack of faded letters. She read from the first one and then looked up at Nick with a tremble in her lips.

"Are these...?"

"From the king to your mother." He nodded to Gideon. "Gid and I found them, with some help from Eloise's personal assistant. I don't think he ever sent them."

Her eyes had taken on a glassy sheen. She hugged the letters to chest. "I can't wait to read them."

Alessandra knew her sister sometimes felt adrift after her mother's death years ago, so hopefully this look into her heritage would answer some questions and give her closure.

Alessandra leaned her shoulder into her husband's.

"That was a wonderful gift for her."

The piles of gifts were dwindling when Gideon slipped his hand over hers. "I think it's about time for our announcement, don't you?"

He stood just as she noticed Pieter getting to his feet, one hand in his hip pocket.

"Gid—"

But her husband had already begun speaking, voice booming in the high-ceilinged room. "Alessandra and I have something to tell you."

He reached for her and drew her up from the sofa. Her face began to heat with excitement and nerves, and she blurted, "We're expecting."

There was a split-second of silence and then the room erupted. She lost sight of Pieter and couldn't tell if he was disappointed—whether they'd ruined his moment again or not.

Mia was the first to descend on them, wrapping both Alessandra and Gideon in an exuberant hug, almost bouncing up and down on her toes as she held them. Penny jumped around her feet, not understanding the excitement but happy to join in the melee. Kylie was there next, with a gentler hug for Alessandra, and then Eloise approached, though Alessandra caught something fragile in her older sister's expression. Cody, Nick, and Ethan had come over to slap Gideon on the back, and Alessandra almost missed the moment when Eloise slipped from the boisterous room, but she caught a flash of her sister's gown as disappeared into the hallway.

When Cody came close to offer a brotherly hug,

she whispered, "Is Eloise all right?"

"I know she's happy for you," he said. " I'll check on her. Congratulations."

He slipped away too, following his wife.

Alessandra settled back on the sofa, surrounded by her family. Things had changed so much since the lonely, distant days before she'd intruded into Gideon's life. Now she was at peace, knowing she was bringing a baby into the world to be surrounded by a family flush with love.

Eloise slipped down the winding stone staircase and outside to the castle's private beach. Sequestered by cliffs on two sides, backed by the castle and beach on one side, it was her favorite escape when life in the castle became too much.

As it had just moments ago.

She was so very happy for her sister. Overjoyed. That was the reason for the tears that wouldn't stem. She just hadn't wanted Alessandra to mistake her tears for anything else. Like grief.

Thus the headlong rush to the beach, without even stopping for her coat.

Last night's storm had paused overnight but now had started up again, dusting everything with a light snow. The sky was slate-gray, laden with clouds. The water was choppy—dark gray waves, some with whitecaps.

Wind whipped her hair into her eyes and chapped her skin. She really should've stopped for a coat.

And then Cody was there, appearing like an apparition through the blowing snow. He wrapped a cloak around her shoulders, enclosing her in warmth.

His arms came around her next, tucking her close to the wall of his chest. He cupped the back of her head.

She pressed her face into the space between his shoulder and neck.

"Your nose is freezing." His voice was a rumble through his chest.

Other than that, he didn't say anything, just held her.

Finally, when her tears had dried, he wiped her cheeks with a handkerchief.

"I'm happy for Alessandra and Gideon," she said with a stubborn lift of her chin.

His gaze searched her face. "Okay," he said slowly. "Then why the tears?"

And everything she'd been holding inside for all these months burst from her lips. "Because *I* want to be expecting too!"

He looked stunned at her exclamation, surprise lifting his brows. "You do?"

They stood close enough that her cloak blew around their legs, and he shared his warmth with her.

He cupped her jaw. Obviously, he was trying to understand. "Every time I've brought up us having a baby, you've pretended you haven't heard me."

"I heard you," she said with another tilt of her chin. "And of course I think about it. Often. It's expected that the Glorvaird monarch will have at least one child."

She took an icy breath. Her lashes were clumping with snowflakes. "I'm just...frightened."

"Of what?"

It was hard to say the words while she was wrapped in his warmth, but she did, pushing them past the lump in her throat. "What if...what if my own child is frightened of my appearance?"

This time the tilt of her chin was downward. She'd grown accustomed to being the public face of the royal family, but mentioning her scars was not natural for her. Not at all.

But as usual, Cody refused to let her hide. He lifted her face to his, his thumb running over the stiff ridges of skin along her cheek and jaw.

"These scars?" he asked. "This sign of your resilience?"

She nodded, the slightly-rough skin of his palm rasping against her cheek.

He bent closer, this time placing butterfly-light kisses along the line of her scars. "These scars?" he asked again. "This sign of your courage?"

A shudder went through her, a whole-body tremble that only intensified when his kisses moved to the sensitive skin just beneath the line of her jaw.

He moved back slightly, waiting until her eyes had learned to focus again. His expression was terribly serious as he looked down on her. "I love you, Eloise. Do you trust me to tell you the truth?"

It took a massive amount of courage, but she nodded.

"When I look at you, I no longer see your scars. You are so beautiful to me."

Tears pricked her eyes once again. What a terribly

romantic thing to say.

"If we are blessed with a child, or two, or ten, I expect they'll see you the very same way I do. They'll think their mother is the most beautiful woman in the world."

She sniffled valiantly.

But he wasn't done. "If, someday, our children ask about your scars, I'll tell them about the heroic, brave, resilient young woman who almost died in a horrific accident but clawed her way to survival, and then, when she had no other choice, came into her own and became a beautiful queen."

She could no longer contain her emotion, and two silent tears slipped down her cheeks.

She threw her arms around his neck, not caring that her cloak had slipped and icy air was sliding down her neck. "I love you. I love you so much!" She peppered his face with kisses. "I've no idea what I did to deserve you—probably I don't—but I'm so glad your uncle tried to steal that jeweled rose."

He chuckled, the sound a comfort to her. Her loyal, wonderful husband. Her heart was full.

"Let's get you back to the castle before you come down with pneumonia." He wrapped one arm around her waist, and she snuggled in close.

"So when should we start trying for all these ten babies?" she teased, content to lean into his strength.

He laughed. "Well, you've got a castle full of family, all in celebrating moods. Probably best to wait until tonight."

She reached up to kiss beneath his ear. "Deal."

He squeezed her waist. "Happy Christmas."

LACY WILLIAMS

Pieter rushed down one of the castle's winding hallways, not paying a bit of attention to where he was going, only needing to escape.

He couldn't breathe. The two carat diamond solitaire in his pocket felt as if it were branding him through his trousers.

His best laid plans were in shambles. He'd had such good intentions...a perfect plan to propose marriage to McKenna. Then everything had gone wrong in one huge spiral. First, the castle staff had mistaken her for a common worker, then she'd been so excited to share her news of being accepting to law school. He'd known that remained her goal. Had even planned for it, asking Eloise to make him a royal ambassador to the United States, so he and McKenna could live there and she could continue her education and then practice law. It hadn't seemed right to preempt her moment of celebration with his proposal.

And then this morning, he'd been on the verge of getting on one knee, thinking that having the family together would make it a meaningful moment. And then Alessandra and Gideon had broken their baby news, and his moment had passed again.

Christmas Day was half over, and his chances of making the proposal perfect were rapidly disappearing.

This was a mess.

He slowed his steps and turned a corner, stopping short when he nearly ran into one of today's skeleton staff, a stout woman at least a head shorter than he.

He recognized her instantly as the head housekeeper, the woman who'd dragged McKenna into service in the kitchen last night.

She recognized him too, her eyes going wide before she dropped into a curtsy.

"Excuse me, sir." She lowered her head and attempted to pass by him.

The lighting wasn't particularly good in the stone hallway, but he could see the puffiness in her eyes and the blotchy spots of red across her face. Something was wrong.

And maybe loving McKenna had softened him. He whirled before she could go. "Wait a moment."

She paused, head and shoulders drooping even lower. "Please don't sack me, sir. I've a ten-year-old daughter at home, and I'm the only source of income for our family."

He grimaced. Perhaps he hadn't shed his old self completely if this is what the staff thought of him.

"I'm not going to sack you. I doubt the queen would allow it, it any case."

She dared to look up.

And the tiny McKenna conscience-angel on his shoulder prodded him until he asked. "I was going to ask if there was anything I could do for you. You seem...upset."

The surprise that crossed her face offended him. Really? Was his reputation so bad, even after years of proving himself? He had half a mind to stomp off, but maybe that was the kind of behavior that had gotten him the reputation in the first place.

"No, sir. There's nothing you can do. I lost my mum last Christmas, and this holiday has been a little emotional for me."

How awful. No wonder she'd been extra stressed last night. McKenna had been kind enough to help out, and her actions had been more of a blessing than she'd even known.

"I'm sorry for your loss," he said, and he meant it. "If you need to go home, I'm sure the queen will understand."

She shook her head slightly. "I asked to work today. My girl is in the kitchens. And I think the distraction might be something of a blessing. Besides, it's a short day."

He nodded. "Happy Christmas to you."

"And to you."

He started to walk off, but her next words stopped him. "Your girl is special," she said. He turned to see her earnest expression. "Last night proved it, at least to me."

"She is." *She is.*

He knew it. Why was he worrying so much about

making the proposal perfect? What mattered to McKenna was that he loved her.

Mission fixed in his mind, he strode back the way he'd come and entered the atrium, where the family was still sitting, talking, and enjoying the holiday. Eloise and Cody rejoined the group from another doorway, clothing slightly damp but beaming.

He hardly paid them any attention as he strode straight to McKenna, where she sat on a settee. The lights from the tree were sparkling and her cheeks were slightly rosy from the champagne they'd sipped earlier after Alessandra and Gideon's announcement. She looked up at him, her smile fading slightly, her eyes narrowing, as he paused in front of her.

He sank to one knee.

His heart thudded deeply in his ears. Even so, he heard the soft intake of her breath. One hand came up to rest over her heart.

He reached into his pocket and pulled out the ring. It sparkled in the light.

The room hushed. It was as though everybody held their breaths.

"McKenna, you are my heart. Being with you has changed me for the better, made me a better man. And I don't ever want to be without you. Will you do me the great honor of becoming my wife?"

She didn't hesitate, a bright smile spreading across her face. "Yes!"

His eyes misted over, and he felt both their hands shaking as he slipped his family crest ring from her finger and replaced it with the engagement ring.

She waited until he'd secured the ring and then threw her arms around his neck. He wobbled on his knee, finally settling the both of them on the sofa she'd occupied. They sealed the deal with a passionate kiss, breaking off only when Gideon cleared his throat.

Pieter shot the man a look as the others interrupted his moment to offer their congratulations. Gideon only smiled back, unrepentant.

It wasn't the perfectly planned proposal he'd imagined, but the important part was that she'd said yes.

This would definitely be a Christmas to hold in their memories forever.

LACY WILLIAMS

ABOUT THE AUTHOR

USA Today bestselling author Lacy Williams works in a hostile environment (read: four kids age 7 and under). In spite of this, she has somehow managed to be a hybrid author since 2011, publishing 34 books & novellas. Lacy's books have finaled in the *RT Book Reviews* Reviewers' Choice Awards (2012, 2013, & 2014), the Golden Quill and the Booksellers Best Award. She is a member of American Christian Fiction Writers, Romance Writers of America and Novelists Inc.